Once Upon A Balloon

by Bree Galbraith

illustrations by Isabelle Malenfant

ORCA BOOK PUBLISHERS

Library and Archives Canada Cataloguing in Publication

Galbraith, Bree, 1981-
Once upon a balloon / Bree Galbraith ; illustrated by Isabelle Malenfant.

Issued also in electronic format.
ISBN 978-1-4598-0324-4

I. Malenfant, Isabelle, 1979- II. Title.
PS8613.A4592063 2013   jc813'.6   C2013-901929-4

First published in the United States, 2013
Library of Congress Control Number: 2013935385

Summary: After accidentally letting go of the string on his balloon, Theo learns from his older brother Zeke where all the lost balloons in the world go.

Orca Book Publishers is dedicated to preserving the environment and has printed this book on Forest Stewardship Council® certified paper.

Orca Book Publishers gratefully acknowledges the support for its publishing programs provided by the following agencies: the Government of Canada through the Canada Book Fund and the Canada Council for the Arts, and the Province of British Columbia through the BC Arts Council and the Book Publishing Tax Credit.

Cover and interior artwork created using watercolor, colored pencil, pastel and numeric colors.

Cover artwork by Isabelle Malenfant
Design by Teresa Bubela

ORCA BOOK PUBLISHERS
PO Box 5626, STN. B
Victoria, BC Canada
V8R 6S4

ORCA BOOK PUBLISHERS
PO Box 468
Custer, WA USA
98240-0468

www.orcabook.com
Printed and bound in Canada.

16 15 14 13 • 4 3 2 1

To Dario and Oakland, the loves of my life.
—B.G.

For Pascal, following the wind up to Chicago.
—I.M.

Theo and Zeke's cousin

gave them four balloons. Zeke took three and handed
Theo one, a small green one with a long orange string.

With all four balloons weaving this way and that, Theo's father had to strain to see out the car's back window. Before they got out of the car, Theo's mom offered to tie Theo's balloon to his wrist. But Theo said no.

"Don't let go of the string," said his mom.

"Don't let go of the string," said his dad.

"Don't let go of the string," said his brother, Zeke. He told Theo that if he did, he wouldn't give him another one because he would waste that one too.

Theo thought Zeke was probably right.

Theo tried to hold on, he really did. He stared at his hand and told it to stay closed, but it didn't want to listen. He clenched his fist so tight, his knuckles turned white, but his fingers had other plans. Theo watched the string slip from his hand. The balloon drifted upward, slowly at first, and then in a hurry.

His brother scowled, his dad shrugged, and his mom sighed.

Higher and higher the balloon rose, past the trees and telephone lines, dodging buildings and birds until it was a tiny speck. And then it was gone. There was no green dot floating against the big blue sky.

Theo knew it must be up there somewhere,
but where?

Inside, Theo's dad was working at the computer.
"Where did my balloon go?" Theo asked.

His dad looked at him and smiled. "The moon.
How else do you think it stays up there?"

Theo didn't believe him.

Theo's mom was painting. He asked her where
his balloon had gone.

"Oh, it probably popped when the air pressure
changed way, way up high," she said.

Theo didn't believe her. But just in case, he went
outside to see if any pieces of popped balloon had
landed on the ground. There was nothing there,
so he went to find his brother.

"Do you know where my balloon is?" he asked his brother.

"Chicago," Zeke said, peering through the tower he had built. "It is a little-known fact that all lost balloons end up in Chicago."

Zeke explained that Chicago was quite far away and was known as the Windy City. Balloons from around the world followed the wind to Chicago. He said it had something to do with science, migration patterns and wind tunnels created by invisible jets.

Then he told Theo about Frank.

Frank was in charge of the balloons that landed in Chicago.
His official title, Nocturnal City Collection Custodian,
was one Frank had held for over thirty-five years.

Night after night, to avoid disturbing the public, Frank
loaded his box of balloon-grabbing tools into his truck.
There was the Pincher, which could grab hold of any
balloon's string; the Fork, useful for combing balloons from
tree branches; and the Hook, best used in hard-to-reach
places. And lastly there was Frank's trusty Twister.

Zeke said Frank was tired and wanted to retire. For ten years the city had posted an ad in the newspaper, looking for a replacement. Not one person had ever applied.

"Frank's boss gave him a night off, once," said Zeke. "But a bunch of 110th-birthday balloons from Japan caused a traffic jam on the highway."

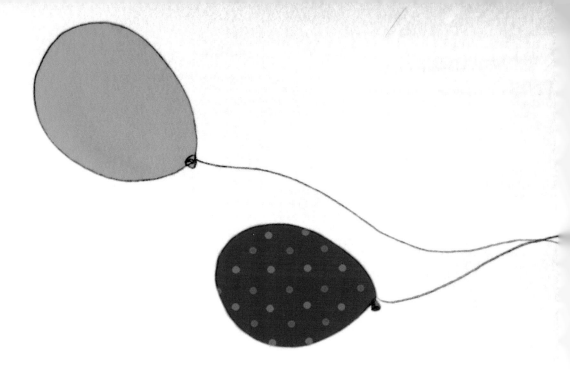

Zeke knew everything about everything, so he knew *everything* about Frank. He said that every night Frank carried a full bag of balloons back to his warehouse. Then he dreamed about creating a robot that could do his job. A robot that wouldn't mind the windy nights and cold winters, when balloons froze to the trees or popped when the temperature dropped.

Inside Frank's warehouse were birthday balloons; baby balloons; graduation and retirement balloons; plain, spotted and polka-dotted balloons.

They drifted above Frank in a big, happy balloon family.

Theo liked the thought of hundreds of balloons hovering above like a big cloud. But Zeke said the balloons only reminded Frank of all the special occasions he had missed due to the odd hours he kept.

"Frank starts every shift at sunset with a cup of coffee and a long sigh," said Zeke. But lately Frank had begun to tinker with the robot parts he had collected. "When he is done tinkering, he starts his truck and circles the city. He finds balloons in trees, balloons on pathways and balloons in fountains. Balloons love fountains."

Zeke told Theo everyone loved Chicago, including Frank.
But by the time Frank arrived anywhere, it was dark and all the
excitement was over. Frank wanted to see the crowds, smell
the hotdogs and hear the children cheer at the big game.

Theo felt sad for Frank, for his loneliness and his long nights.
He wanted to tell Frank to go ahead and build the robot, and that
his mom said if you believe in yourself, you can do anything.

He wanted to tell Frank all of this, but he didn't know how.
So in the morning he asked his brother.

Zeke was certain there was only one way to get a message to Frank. He grabbed one of his three balloons, an orange one, and told Theo to hold it between his hands. Then Zeke took a thick black marker and wrote a message on the balloon.

Dear Frank, it said. *Good luck with your robot. From Zeke and Theo.*

The brothers went outside and let the balloon go. It floated away, dodging trees, buildings and birds, drifting in the breeze until it disappeared.

Zeke said it was lucky they had an orange balloon because orange balloons are faster than any other color of balloon. It would only take a day for their message to reach Chicago.

That evening as the boys were getting ready for bed, Theo said he hoped the balloon hadn't popped when the air pressure changed.

Zeke told Theo not to believe everything he heard.

Theo climbed into bed. "Zeke, has our balloon made it to Chicago yet?" he asked.

Zeke said that after Frank had finished his coffee and loaded his tools into his truck, he spotted their bright orange balloon stuck in a tree. "He pulled Twister out and brought the balloon down. And when he read our message, for the first time in a long time, Frank smiled."

Zeke said Frank was happy because finally one of the balloons was for him.

With their balloon in hand, Frank made his way back
to the warehouse. He spent the rest of the night doing
what he should have done a long time ago. He tinkered
and tinkered until his robot was no longer a dream.